Jump Back, Honey

The Poems of Paul Laurence Dunbar

ILLUSTRATIONS BY

Ashley Bryan

Carole Byard

Jan Spivey Gilchrist

Brian Pinkney

Jerry Pinkney

Faith Ringgold

Jump at the Sun/Hyperion Books for Children New York

FIRST EDITION
1 3 5 7 9 10 8 6 4 2

LIBRARY OF CONGRESS CATALOGING-IN-PUBLICATION DATA
Dunbar, Paul Laurence, 1872–1906.
[Poems. Selections]
Jump Back, Honey: poems/by Paul Laurence Dunbar; selected and with an introduction by Ashley Bryan and Andrea Davis Pinkney; illustrations by Ashley Bryan . . . [et al.]—1st ed.   p. cm.
Summary: An illustrated collection of poems by Paul Laurence Dunbar, including "A Boy's Summer Song," "The Sparrow," and "Little Brown Baby."
ISBN 0-7868-0464-5—ISBN 0-7868-2406-9 (lib. bdg.)
1. Afro-Americans—Juvenile poetry. 2. Children's poetry, American. [1. Afro-Americans—Poetry. 2. American poetry.] I. Bryan, Ashley, ill. II. Pinkney, Andrea Davis. III. Title.
PS1556.A4 1999   811'.4-dc21 98-54252

PAUL LAURENCE DUNBAR

At the turn of the century, one of America's most famous writers was the poet Paul Laurence Dunbar. He was born on June 27, 1872, in Dayton, Ohio, the son of former slaves.

In Central High School, Paul Laurence Dunbar was the only Black student in his class. His poems began to appear in school and local newspapers, and he became known as a writer. He was admitted to the school's literary society and, in his senior year, was elected president of this society and editor of the school paper.

Dunbar wrote the lyrics for the class song, which were set to music by the music teacher and sung at the commencement exercises. After graduating from high school, he would have liked to attend college, but it was out of the question. His mother, Matilda, had worked hard to see him through high school, and he wished to make things easier for her.

One of Dunbar's first jobs was running an elevator in a downtown building. He kept a notebook handy on the job and between calls jotted down ideas and worked on poems.

In late December of 1892, Paul Laurence Dunbar's first book of poetry, *Oak and Ivy,* was published, thanks to the kindness of William L. Blocher, the business manager of the United Brethren Publishing House in Dayton.

Dunbar's work brought him national attention. He was both praised and criticized for his poems written in Black dialect.

Dunbar himself did not speak in dialect, nor did those closest to him. Even Paul's mother had a hard time understanding why her son would choose to write poems in "plantation talk." She had worked hard to get rid of the "slave dialect" in her own speech. And she loved to brag about her son's ability to speak perfect English. But Paul found an important outlet for his lively wit and love of characterization in his use of dialect.

Paul's poem "Little Brown Baby" has become an American classic. Written in Black dialect, "Little Brown Baby" was created out of Paul's childhood memories of his father. When Paul was a child, his father often called him over and invited young Paul to sit on his lap. He would then tell Paul exciting stories that he often made up on the spot. Sometimes the stories were mysterious thrillers that featured "de big buggah-man" who could appear at any moment. "Little Brown Baby" shows the special love a father has for his child. It is a poem that appeals to parents and children of all races.

Paul took many odd jobs to support the meager earnings he made as a poet. In the spring of 1893, he found a job as a waiter in a Chicago restaurant. As always, Paul carefully observed people and listened to their ways of speaking. In the restaurant, the other waiters had a code. They came and went from the kitchen to the dining room through a swinging door. To keep from bumping into each other—and to avoid the risk of spilling trays of food—the waiters would call out, "Jump back, honey, jump back," as they approached the swinging door.

The waiters' lively, repetitive rhythms inspired Paul to write "A Negro Love Song." Although the poem originated in the hubbub of a busy restaurant, it has blossomed into a playful courting poem that has, for decades, enticed lovers to the dance floor. "A Negro Love Song" can also be heard on the playground as a jump rope chant.

For nearly a century, schoolchildren everywhere have come to cherish Paul Laurence Dunbar's poetry. Many can cite it line and verse in the classroom, at church, with friends, and at bedtime. A favorite with younger children is "Dawn," a poem that beautifully captures the quiet mystery of a new day.

The poems in this book were chosen carefully for their appeal to children, and for the purpose of offering young readers a range of Dunbar's poetic styles, both in standard English and in dialect. Brought vibrantly to life by some of the most beloved African-American illustrators of our time, *Jump Back, Honey* is meant to spark the poetic imagination of all who read it.

To that aim Dunbar himself would surely say: "Amen!"

—ASHLEY BRYAN AND ANDREA DAVIS PINKNEY

Ashley Bryan

Dawn

An angel, robed in spotless white,
Bent down and kissed the sleeping Night.
Night woke to blush; the sprite was gone.
Men saw the blush and called it Dawn.

Ashley Bryan

Spring Song

A blue-bell springs upon the ledge,
A lark sits singing in the hedge;
Sweet perfumes scent the balmy air,
And life is brimming everywhere.
What lark and breeze and bluebird sing,
      Is Spring, Spring, Spring!

No more the air is sharp and cold;
The planter wends across the wold,
And glad beneath the shining sky
We wander forth, my love and I.
And ever in our hearts doth ring
      This song of Spring, Spring!

For life is life and love is love,
'Twixt maid and man or dove and dove.
Life may be short, life may be long,
But love will come, and to its song
Shall this refrain for ever cling
      Of Spring, Spring, Spring!

Ashley Bryan

A Boy's Summer Song

'Tis fine to play
In the fragrant hay,
And romp on the golden load;
To ride old Jack
To the barn and back,
Or tramp by a shady road.
To pause and drink,
At a mossy brink;
Ah, that is the best of joy,
And so I say
On a summer's day,
What's so fine as being a boy?
Ha, Ha!

With line and hook
By a babbling brook,
The fisherman's sport we ply;
And list the song
Of the feathered throng
That flit in the branches nigh.
At last we strip
For a quiet dip;
Ah, that is the best of joy.
For this I say
On a summer's day,
What's so fine as being a boy?
Ha, Ha!

Ashley Bryan

Faith Ringgold

Morning

The mist has left the greening plain,
The dew-drops shine like fairy rain,
The coquette rose awakes again
    Her lovely self adorning.
The Wind is hiding in the trees,
A sighing, soothing, laughing tease,
Until the rose says "Kiss me, please,"
    'Tis morning, 'tis morning.

With staff in hand and careless-free
The wanderer fares right jauntily,
For towns and houses are, thinks he,
    For scorning, for scorning.
My soul is swift upon the wing,
And in its deeps a song I bring;
Come, Love, and we together sing,
    "'Tis morning, 'tis morning."

Douglass

Ah, Douglass, we have fall'n on evil days,
    Such days as thou, not even thou didst know,
    When thee, the eyes of that harsh long ago
Saw, salient, at the cross of devious ways,
And all the country heard thee with amaze.
    Not ended then, the passionate ebb and flow,
    The awful tide that battled to and fro;
We ride amid a tempest of dispraise.

Now, when the waves of swift dissension swarm,
    And Honor, the strong pilot, lieth stark,
Oh, for thy voice high-sounding o'er the storm,
    For thy strong arm to guide the shivering bark,
The blast-defying power of thy form,
    To give us comfort through the lonely dark.

Faith Ringgold

Carole Byard

The Sparrow

A little bird, with plumage brown,
Beside my window flutters down,
A moment chirps its little strain,
Then taps upon my window-pane,
And chirps again, and hops along,
To call my notice to its song;
But I work on, nor heed its lay,
Till, in neglect, it flies away.

So birds of peace and hope and love
Come fluttering earthward from above,
To settle on life's window-sills,
And ease our load of earthly ills;
But we, in traffic's rush and din
Too deep engaged to let them in,
With deadened heart and sense plod on,
Nor know our loss till they are gone.

The Farm Child's Lullaby

Oh, the little bird is rocking in the cradle of the wind,
     And it's bye, my little wee one, bye;
The harvest all is gathered and the pippins all are binned;
      Bye, my little wee one, bye;
The little rabbit's hiding in the golden shock of corn,
The thrifty squirrel's laughing bunny's idleness to scorn;
You are smiling with the angels in your slumber, smile till morn;
     So it's bye, my little wee one, bye.

There'll be plenty in the cellar, there'll be plenty on the shelf;
     Bye, my little wee one, bye;
There'll be goodly store of sweetings for a dainty little elf;
     Bye, my little one, bye.
The snow may be a-flying o'er the meadow and the hill,
The ice has checked the chatter of the little laughing rill,
But in your cosy cradle, you are warm and happy still;
     So bye, my little wee one, bye.

Why, the Bob White thinks, the snowflake is a brother to his
          song;
     Bye, my little wee one, bye;
And the chimney sings the sweeter when the wind is blowing
          strong;
     Bye, my little wee one, bye;
The granary's overflowing, full is cellar, crib, and bin,
The wood has paid its tribute and the ax has ceased its din;
The winter may not harm you when you're sheltered safe within;
     So bye, my little wee one, bye.

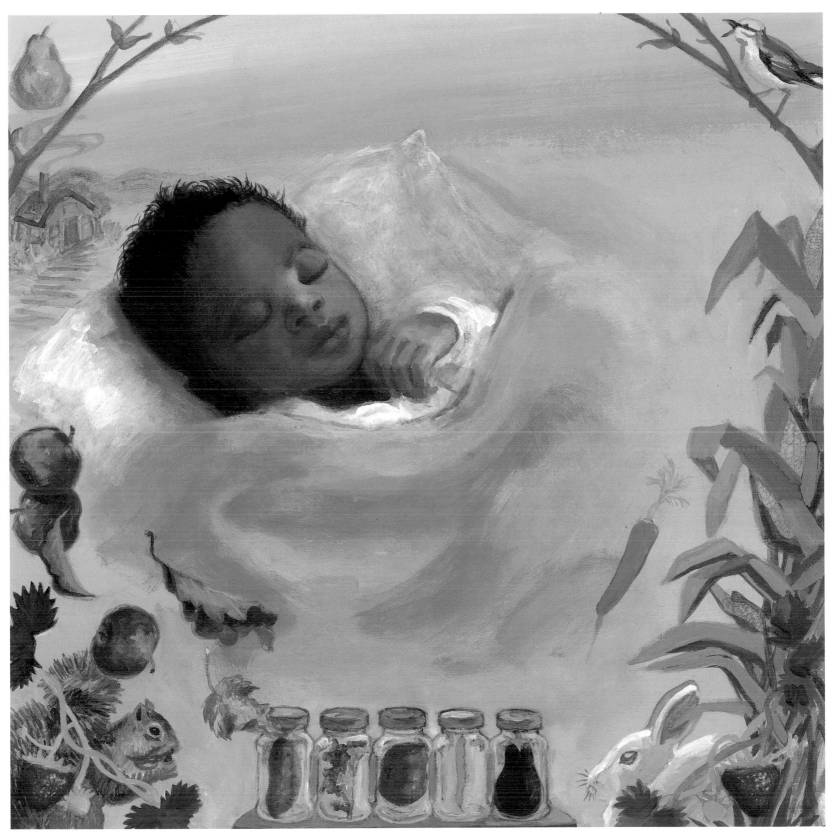

Carole Byard

Jerry Pinkney

A Negro Love Song

Seen my lady home las' night,
　　　Jump back, honey, jump back.
Hel' huh han' an' sque'z it tight,
　　　Jump back, honey, jump back.
Hyeahd huh sigh a little sigh
Seen a light gleam f'om huh eye,
An' a smile go flittin' by—
　　　Jump back, honey, jump back.

Hyeahd de win' blow thoo de pine,
　　　Jump back, honey, jump back.
Mockin'-bird was singin' fine,
　　　Jump back, honey, jump back.
An' my hea't was beatin' so,
When I reached my lady's do',
Dat I couldn't ba' to go—
　　　Jump back, honey, jump back.

Put my ahm aroun' huh wais',
　　　Jump back, honey, jump back.
Raised huh lips an' took a tase,
　　　Jump back, honey, jump back.
Love me, honey, love me true?
Love me well ez I love you?
An' she answe'd, "Cose I do"—
　　　Jump back, honey, jump back.

Jerry Pinkney

The Colored Band

W'en de colo'ed ban' comes ma'chin' down de street,
Don't you people stan' daih starin'; lif' yo' feet!
    Ain't dey playin'? Hip, hooray!
    Stir yo' stumps an' cleah de way,
Fu' de music dat dey mekin' can't be beat.

Oh, de major man's a-swingin' of his stick,
An' de pickaninnies crowdin' roun' him thick'
        In his go'geous uniform,
        He's de lightnin' of de sto'm,
An' de little clouds erroun' look mighty slick.

You kin hyeah a fine perfo'mance w'en de white ban's
        serenade,
        An' dey play dey high-toned music mighty sweet,
But hit's Sousa played in ragtime, an' hit's Rastus on
        Parade
        We'n de colo'ed ban' comes ma'chin' down de street.

We'n de colo'ed ban' comes ma'chin down de street
You kin hyeah de ladies all erroun' repeat:
        "Ain't dey handsome? Ain't dey gran'?
        Ain't dey splendid? Goodness lan'!
W'y dey's pu'fect f'om dey fo'heads to dey feet!"

An' sich steppin' to de music down de line,
'T ain't de music by itself dat makes it fine,
        Hit's de walkin', step by step,
        An' de keepin' time wid "Hep,"
Dat it mek a common ditty soun' divine.

Oh, de white ban' play hit's music, an hit's mighty good
        to hyeah,
An' it sometimes leaves a ticklin' in yo' feet;
But be hea't goes into bus'ness fu' to he'p erlong de eah,
        We'n de colo'ed ban' goes ma'chin' down de street.

When Malindy Sings

G'way an'quit dat noise, Miss Lucy—
    Put dat music book away;
What's de use to keep on tryin'?
    Ef you practise twell you're gray,
You cain't sta't no notes a-flyin'
    Lak de ones dat rants and rings
F'om de kitchen to de big woods
    When Malindy sings.

You ain't got de nachel o' gans
    Fu' to make de soun' come right,
You ain't got de tu'ns an' twistin's,
    Fu' to make it sweet an' light.
Tell you one thing now, Miss Lucy,
    An' I'm tellin' you fu' true,
When it comes to raal right singin',
    'T ain't no easy thing to do.

Easy 'nough fu' folks to hollah,
    Lookin' at de lines an' dots,
When dey ain't no one kin sence it,
    An' de chune comes in, in spots;
But fu' real melojous music,
    Dat jes' strikes yo' hea't an' clings,
Jes' you stan' an' listen wif me
    When Malindy sings.

Ain't you nevah hyeahd Malindy?
　　Blessed soul, tek up de cross!
Look hyeah, ain't you jokin' honey?
　　Well, you don't know what you los'.
Y'ought to hyeah dat gal a-wablin',
　　Robins, la'ks an all dem things,
Heish dey moufs an' hides dey faces
　　When Malindy sings.

Fiddlin' man jes' stop his fiddlin',
　　Lay his fiddle on de she'f;
Mockin'-bird quit tryin' to whistle,
　　'Cause he jes' so shamed hisse'f.
Folks a-playin' on de banjo
　　Draps dey fingahs on de strings—
Bless yo' soul—fu'gits to move em,
　　When Malindy sings.

She jes' spreads huh mouf and hollahs,
　　"Come to Jesus," twell you hyeah
Sinnahs' tremblin' steps and voices
　　Timid-lak a-drawin' neah;
Den she tu'ns to "Rock of Ages,"
　　Simply to de cross she clings,
An' you fin' yo' teahs a-drappin'
　　When Malindy sings.

Who dat says dat humble praises
　　Wif de Master nevah counts?
Heish yo' mouf, I hyeah dat music,
　　Ez hit rises up an' mounts—
Floatin' by de hills an' valleys,
　　Way above dis buryin' sod,
Ez hit makes its way in glory
　　To de very gates of God!

Oh, hit's sweetah dan de music
　　Oh an edicated band;
An' hit's dearah dan de battle's
　　Song o' triumph in de lan'.
It seems holier dan evenin'
　　When de solemn chu'ch bell rings,
Ez I sit an' ca'mly listen
　　While Malindy sings.

Towsah, stop dat ba'kin', hyeah me!
　　Mandy, mek dat chile keep still;
Don't you hyeah de echoes callin'
　　F'om de valley to de hill?
Let me listen, I can hyeah it,
　　Th'oo de bresh of angels' wings,
Sof' an' sweet, "Swing Low, Sweet Chariot,"
　　Ez Malindy sings.

Brian Pinkney

Little Brown Baby

Little brown baby wif spa'klin' eyes,
    Come to yo' pappy an' set on his knee.
What you been doin', suh—makin' san' pies?
    Look at dat bib—you's ez du'ty ez me.
Look at dat mouf—dat's merlasses, I bet;
    Come hyeah, Maria, an' wipe off his han's.
Bees gwine to ketch you an' eat you up yit,
    Bein' so sticky an' sweet—goodness lan's!

Little brown baby wif spa'klin' eyes,
    Who's pappy's darlin' an' who's pappy's chile?
Who is it all de day nevah once tries
    Fu' to be cross, er once loses dat smile?
Whah did you git dem teef? My you's a scamp!
    Whah did dat dimple come f'om in yo' chin?
Pappy do' know you—I b'lieves you's a tramp;
    Mammy, dis' hyeah's some ol' straggler got in!

Let's th'ow him outen de do' in de san',
    We do' want stragglers a-layin' 'roun' hyeah;
Let's gin him 'way to de big buggah-man;
    I know he's hidin' erroun' hyeah right neah.
Buggah-man, buggah-man, come in de do',
    Hyeah's a bad boy you can have fu' to eat.
Mammy an' pappy do' want him no mo',
    Swaller him down f'om his haid to his feet!

Dah, now, I t'ought dat you'd hug me up close.
　　Go back, ol' buggah, you sha'n't have dis boy.
He ain't no tramp, ner no straggler of co'se;
　　He's pappy's pa'dner an' playmate an' joy.
Come to you' pallet now—go to yo' res';
　　Wisht you could allus know ease an' cleah skies;
Wisht you could stay jus' a chile on my breas'—
　　Little brown baby wif spa'klin' eyes!

Brian Pinkney

Good-Night

The lark is silent in his nest,
    The breeze is sighing in its flight,
Sleep, Love, and peaceful be thy rest.
    Good-night, my love, good-night, good-night.

Sweet dreams attend thee in thy sleep,
    To soothe thy rest till morning's light,
And angels round thee vigil keep.
    Good-night, my love, good-night, good-night.

Sleep well, my love, on night's dark breast,
    And ease thy soul with slumber bright;
Be joy but thine and I am blest.
    Good-night my love, good-night, good-night.

Jan Spivey Gilchrist

The Sand-Man

I know a man
With a face of tan
But who is ever kind;
Whom girls and boys
Leave games and toys
Each eventide to find.

When day grows dim,
They watch for him,
He comes his place to claim;
He wears the crown
Of Dreaming-town;
The sand-man is his name.

When sparkling eyes
Troop sleepywise
And busy lips grow dumb;
When little heads
Nod toward the beds,
We know the sand-man's come.

Jan Spivey Gilchrist

Jan Spivey Gilchrist

Rain-Songs

The rain streams down like harp-strings from the sky;
The wind, that world-old harpist sitteth by;
And ever as he sings his low refrain,
He plays upon the harp-strings of the rain.

ABOUT THE ARTISTS

Here, each artist shares memories and muses of Paul Laurence Dunbar.

Ashley Bryan's tempera and gouache paintings illustrate the poems "Dawn," "Spring Song," and "A Boy's Summer Song." Mr. Bryan is the distinguished author and illustrator of numerous books for children, including *Ashley Bryan's ABC of African-American Poetry*, for which he won a Coretta Scott King Honor Award, and *Beat the Story Drum, Pum-Pum*, which won the Coretta Scott King Award. Mr. Bryan was a professor of art at Dartmouth College for many years. He now lives in Islesford, Maine.

"Growing up in New York City in the 1930s, the work of Black American poets was not introduced in my school studies. It was through my love of poetry that I discovered Paul Laurence Dunbar and other Black American poets. I then sought out Dunbar's collected poems, and was struck by his artistic range—everything from dialect poems to lyrical poems in standard English. Since his dialect poems were widely available, I later published *I Greet the Dawn*, a book of Dunbar's poems that emphasized his contributions to standard English poetry."

Carole Byard's distinguished oil paintings illustrate the poems "The Sparrow" and "The Farm Child's Lullaby." Ms. Byard is a fine artist and illustrator whose books for children have twice won the Coretta Scott King Award. *Working Cotton* by Sherley Anne Williams received the Caldecott Honor Medal. Ms. Byard is a lecturer at New York City's Parsons School of Design. She lives in Kerhonkson, New York.

"When I was a child, Paul Laurence Dunbar was never read in our house—he was *performed*, mostly by my aunt Mimi, whose favorite poem was 'In the Morning.' Another family favorite was 'The Party'—a hilarious performance by my aunt Ninna. When she recited, everyone laughed till they cried. My earliest and fondest memory of Paul Laurence Dunbar is of my father reaching for me and saying, 'Little brown baby with spa'k-lin' eyes . . . come to yo' pappy an' set on his knee . . .' I love Paul Laurence Dunbar for these precious memories."

Jan Spivey Gilchrist uses acrylic and oil to illustrate the poems "Good-Night," "The Sand-Man," and "Rain-Songs." Ms. Gilchrist is a celebrated children's book illustrator with several acclaimed books to her credit, including *Angels* and *Easter Parade*, both by Eloise Greenfield. Ms. Gilchrist was chosen as the 1998 Children's Illustrator of the Year by the Chicago Black History Month Book Fair and Conference Salute to African-Americans in Publishing. She lives in Olympia Fields, Illinois.

"I remember the words of Paul Laurence Dunbar echoing throughout the walls of the many churches and community centers where my father, Reverend Charles Spivey, worked with programs featuring children. Mr.

Dunbar's beautiful, rhythmic words were the perfect way for my friends and I to enjoy and perform poetry and prose depicting African-American life."

Brian Pinkney's distinctive scratchboard, luma dyes, and acrylic paintings illustrate the poems "When Malindy Sings" and "Little Brown Baby." Mr. Pinkney is the illustrator of many acclaimed books for children, including *Duke Ellington*, by Andrea Davis Pinkney, winner of the Caldecott Honor Medal and the Coretta Scott King Honor Award. *The Faithful Friend* by Robert D. San Souci also received the Caldecott Honor Medal. Mr. Pinkney is the recipient of three Coretta Scott King Honor Awards and the Boston Globe/Horn Book Award. He lives in Brooklyn, New York.

"When I was starting out as an illustrator, I attended a literacy conference, where I met Patricia McKissack, the distinguished children's book author. This was our first meeting, and we hit it off right away. Soon the conversation turned to African-American children's literature. Without missing a beat, Patricia recited—from memory—Dunbar's 'Little Brown Baby.' After she'd finished, she turned to me and said, 'You should illustrate this poem someday.' Though Dunbar writes about a father and son, I couldn't help but depict my daughter and myself enjoying a loving moment."

Jerry Pinkney uses pencil and watercolor to illustrate the poems "A Negro Love Song" and "The Colored Band." Mr. Pinkney's many stunning books include *Sam and the Tigers* by Julius Lester, *Minty: A Story of Young Harriet Tubman* by Alan Schroeder, and Gloria Jean Pinkney's *The Sunday Outing* and *Back Home*. Mr. Pinkney is a three-time recipient of the Caldecott Honor Medal. He is the winner of several Coretta Scott King and Coretta Scott King Honor Awards. He lives in Croton-on-Hudson, New York.

"Years ago, my brother-in-law, Kelly, gave me a wonderful gift—*The Life and Works of Paul Laurence Dunbar* by Lida Keck Wiggins. When I showed the book to the mother of a friend, she immediately offered to read aloud from one of Dunbar's dialect poems. The music of her whimsical inflection mesmerized everyone in the room. From that moment to this, I have been a lover of Dunbar's work."

Faith Ringgold's painted story quilts illustrate the poems "Morning" and "Douglass." Ms. Ringgold's work is exhibited in major museums around the world. Her first children's book, *Tar Beach*, won a Caldecott Honor Medal and a Coretta Scott King Award. Ms. Ringgold is the author and illustrator of many books, including *Dinner at Aunt Connie's House* and *Bonjour, Lonnie*. She is a professor of art at the University of California in San Diego. She lives in Englewood, New Jersey.

"One of my favorite Paul Laurence Dunbar poems is 'We Wear the Mask.' I first heard this stirring piece when I was a young girl attending Bible school, and I have loved it ever since. It is so beautiful, so full of sadness and truth. I've always taken such pride in the fact that Paul Laurence Dunbar had an apartment building, The Dunbar Houses, in Harlem, named after him. During the Harlem Renaissance a lot of famous people lived there."